Ruby Rogers
Would You Believe It?

Sue Limb

Illustrations by Bernice Lum

BLOOMSBURY

First published in Great Britain in 2008 by Bloomsbury Publishing Plc
36 Soho Square, London, WID 3QY

A CIP catalogue record of this book is available from the British Library

ISBN 978 0 7475 9245 7

All papers used by Bloomsbury Publishing are natural, recyclable
products made from wood grown in well-managed forests.
The manufacturing processes conform to the environmental
regulations of the country of origin.

Printed in Great Britain by Clays Ltd, St Ives Plc

1 3 5 7 9 10 8 6 4 2

www.suelimbbooks.co.uk
www.bloomsbury.com

CHAPTER 1
I hate you

'WHEN DOES THE Easter bunny actually come?' I asked. 'What day?'

I couldn't remember what had happened last year. Easter is so confusing. You hear the grown-ups saying things like, 'Easter's late this year, isn't it?' Why does Easter have to move around all the time? How can it be late? It's not a bus.

'The Easter Bunny's not coming at all this year,' said Joe. 'He had rabbitosis and had to be put down.' He grinned at me through a mouthful of pasta. 'Easter Bunny Dies,' he went on in his news headlines voice. 'Thousands Mourn. Statue Planned for Trafalgar Square, Next to Nelson.'

'Shut up, Joe, you beast!' I yelled. 'Tell him to stop it, Dad!'

'Stop it, Dad,' said Dad with a silly smile. Sometimes the males in our family gang up on me.

'Easter Bunny to Be Made into Sacred Pie,' Joe went on, pulling a mock solemn face.

'Would he be buried, do you think, or stuffed?' asked Dad horridly.

'Tell them to shut up, Mum!' I pleaded.

'Yes, shut up, the pair of you!' snapped Mum, quite savagely. It surprised me. She looked really grim and she hadn't touched her pasta yet. Maybe something was on her mind. Maybe she was cross with me. Maybe I'd done something wrong without even noticing.

'I wonder how many eggs I'll get,' I said, trying to change the subject into something casual and entertaining. 'One will do, because I hate it when people at school boast about how many eggs they've had.'

I wanted Mum to think I was sensible and didn't want lots of eggs. Secretly, of course, I wouldn't mind having loads. But looking for them in the

garden is more fun than eating them afterwards. I'm not sure why.

'If I do have just one,' I said, 'I hope it's not hollow. That's a rip-off. I'd rather have one of those little ones that are full of yellow and white slime. Sort of sweet slime, you know, kind of like cream.'

'For goodness sake, Ruby, shut up about Easter eggs!' said Mum. I was a bit shocked. She looked pale and cross. But Joe hadn't noticed.

'I haven't got a sweet tooth at all, as everybody knows,' he said. 'My ideal egg would be filled with bacon, tomato and fried onions. With a dash of hot red sauce. And, of course, fried egg with lots of crozzly crusty bits.'

Suddenly Mum jumped up. Joe sort of cringed, as if he thought she was going to hit him or something, even though Mum and Dad never, ever hit us.

But Mum didn't hit anybody. She ran out of the room, charged up the stairs, flew into the bathroom and shut the door with a slam. Then there was the horrid but unmistakable sound of somebody being sick.

We all just sat and stared at one another. Dad got up, went over to the CD player and pressed a button. Some samba music came out. Then Dad went upstairs, leaving Joe and me to look at each other.

'I don't want this now,' I said, putting down my fork. 'That's so gross.'

'On the contrary, it's only given me an appetite,' said Joe. 'I'll have yours if you like.' And he picked up my plate and tipped all my remaining pasta on to his. I stared at him in disgust.

'How can you eat at a time like this?' I asked. My friend Froggo was sick on a school trip once, on the bus, and I couldn't touch my sandwiches all day. Joe looked at his watch.

'Seven thirty,' he said. 'A perfect time to eat in my view. Pass the grated cheese. I want to make my pasta look even more like a plate of sick.'

I passed the grated cheese and stared at him in amazement. He really was eating away cheerfully, as if nothing had happened.

'Why did Dad switch on the music?' I asked.

'So Mum could be sick Latin-American style.'

'Boys are useless,' I said. 'They have no sympathy or anything. In my view you're not even human.'

'There's nothing like samba music to get me going,' said Joe. And he started to eat in time to the music: *bite, chomp-chomp-chomp*. It would have been really funny if we weren't in the middle of this horrible drama.

Mum's hardly ever ill. Nothing like this had happened before. I felt as if I would never be able to eat again, ever. How could Joe just go on filling his face, the insensitive pig?

'I hate you,' I said quietly and with as much poison as I could manage. 'You don't deserve to be a member of this family.'

Dad came back into the room. He was smiling, but it was the sort of smile which grown-ups put on when there's not very much to smile about.

'Mum's fine,' said Dad. 'Just something didn't quite agree with her, that's all. Now who's going to help me clear up in time to the music?'

He broke into a stupid little jiggling dance. It's

bad enough seeing your parents dance anyway –
somehow the most embarrassing thing in the
whole world. But when they start to dance to distract you from something real and horrible that's
happening, it's ten times worse.

'Where's Mum?' I asked, getting down from the
table. 'Is she all right?'

'She's just having a little lie down,' said Dad.
'Normal service will be resumed as soon as possible.'

An idea flashed across my mind. Mum wasn't
OK! She'd *died* up there, but Dad couldn't bear to
tell us. So he was doing all this stupid grinning and

dancing and stuff to try to cheer us up before the dreadful news.

'I'm going to see her!' I said, and ran upstairs.

'Ruby, no!' called Dad, but I took no notice. I had to see Mum. This was like a terrible nightmare.

I burst into Mum's bedroom. She was lying on the bed, facing away from me. I ran around to the other side. Her face was really pale, but she smiled at me. Thank goodness! She was still alive.

She wasn't her usual bubbly self, though. Her smile was kind of thin and pretend.

'Sorry about that, Ruby love,' she said. 'I don't know what came over me. I feel better now. I'm just going to lie down for a bit. Help Dad with the clearing up downstairs, there's a good girl.'

I climbed on to the bed and kissed her. Then I got down and went out.

The whole world seemed kind of sick and nasty, and I knew it wouldn't feel right again until Mum was back to normal.

CHAPTER 2
Amaaaaaaazing!

NEXT MORNING MUM rang in to take the day off work. The rest of us were having our breakfast. Well, Joe and Dad were. They were eating toast. I'd got a bowl of muesli, but I wasn't enjoying it much. I was only on my second mouthful and already I didn't want any more. Round and round and round it went in my mouth, like concrete in a cement mixer but not nearly so tasty.

'I was up half the night, Julie,' Mum was saying to her team leader. 'I've got an appointment to see

Dr Davies this afternoon. She couldn't fit me in this morning.'

I stared at my muesli. It was horrible. I'd never realised before how much it looks like compost. Dad's got a compost heap in the garden and all our kitchen waste goes in there: tea leaves, coffee grounds, apple peelings, the lot.

Actually my muesli looked a lot less appealing than the compost heap. I began to suspect it was made of dirty old toenails, used sticking plaster, mashed-up shoelaces from smelly trainers . . . I pushed my bowl away.

'Can't eat it,' I said.

Dad shrugged. Joe grabbed my bowl and in three massive gulps it was gone. Mum was still on the phone.

'Thanks, Julie. I'm so sorry, I don't know what's the matter with me,' she said.

I glared at Joe. 'I was going to give that to my robins,' I said coldly.

'Haven't seen your robins recently,' said Joe. 'And the new people next door have got a massive ginger cat. Hmmm.' He pulled a *bad news* face.

I felt a pang of horror and ran to the window. Not my robins! I couldn't see a cat anywhere. I ran outside.

Right away the robins arrived: some on the fence, some on the birdtable. I realised I hadn't put their food out this morning. I'd been so miserable about Mum being ill that I'd forgotten all about them.

I rushed indoors, grabbed a plastic scoop of bird food and took it out. I scattered some of it on the ground and put the rest on the bird table. The robins thanked me with cute little flutters and beady eyes. For a split second I felt a bit better.

But when I got indoors Mum had gone upstairs again. Dad was packing up his things.

'Come on, Ruby, or you'll be late for school.'

'Where's Mum?'

'She's just got a little pain. Don't worry, she's seeing the doctor later today and it'll all be sorted out.' Dad grinned and then started to whistle as he put on his jacket. I knew that whistle. He only ever does it when he's really worried.

When I got to school, I looked for Yasmin. You need your best mate at a time like this. But I couldn't see her anywhere. Instead Froggo and Max came up, laughing. It was no use telling them about my mum being ill. Boys can't deal with that kind of stuff.

'Hey, Ruby!' said Froggo. 'I've got a riddle specially for you!'

I like Froggo. He's my best friend who happens to be a boy. I like Max too. He's tall and weird and gets funny ideas sometimes. He's also obsessed with aeroplanes, but I suppose if you're a boy, you have to be.

'What riddle?' I asked.

'Why did the police arrest a bird?' asked Froggo, grinning. I shrugged.

'I dunno.'

'Because he was a robin!' laughed Froggo. He knows about my tame robins. He came to tea last week and helped me feed them.

'A-robbin' – geddit?' said Max. 'Ha ha!' It did make me smile a bit. 'I've got one now!' Max went on. 'What kind of horse never comes out in the daytime?'

'What, then?' I asked.

'A nightmare!'

Just then Lauren came up. She lives on a farm and she actually has her own pony called Charlie, so we told her the nightmare riddle right away. For a moment it looked as if she didn't get it, but then, slowly, a big smile spread over her face.

'That's your own special riddle,' said Froggo. 'Because you're horsey.'

'There's another one for Lauren,' said Max. 'What sort of food do racehorses eat?'

'I don't know,' said Lauren shyly, fiddling with her big clouds of hair.

'Fast food! Hahahahaha!' laughed Max.

At last Yasmin arrived. She was frowning slightly and looking nervous.

'Hey, Yas!' said Froggo. 'Max and I have got riddles off the internet. There's one for everybody. Ruby's is about a robin and Lauren's about horses. What one would suit Yasmin?' He turned to Max.

'I know!' said Max, jumping up and down as if he was skipping. 'What animal talks the most?'

'What?' said Yasmin, sounding a bit cross, as if all this riddle stuff was the stupidest thing ever and she just didn't have time for it at all.

'The yak!' yelled Max.

Yasmin went bright red and looked really offended.

'You can talk!' I snapped. 'You're the one who's always yakking. Plus you have porridge instead of a brain!'

Max made the sound of a jet aircraft screaming across the sky and flew off across the schoolyard with his arms outstretched.

'Why are mosquitoes so annoying?' asked Froggo.

'Why are *you* so annoying, you mean!' snapped Yasmin. 'Come on Ruby – Lauren – leave the idiots to their stupid riddles. Boys! Huh!'

Lauren and I and Yasmin strode off, arm in arm.

'Oh my God, guys!' said Yasmin, as soon as we were by ourselves. 'I'm really, really nervous.'

'Why?' I wanted to tell them about my mum being ill and for a moment it seemed as if Yasmin had stolen the centre stage – as usual.

'I've got to give my talk today! Have you forgotten? The multi-faith project thingy. I've got to give my talk on Islam. Oh my God! I am sooooo nervous! My legs are, like, shaking. Look!'

'You'll be brilliant,' said Lauren. 'You're always so confident, Yasmin. Don't worry. It'll be fine.'

I could understand how nervous Yasmin was, but now I'd started thinking about Mum again, this school stuff seemed a bit unreal.

'Ruby!' said Yasmin suddenly. Even though she was so focussed on her talk, she'd noticed right away that there was something wrong with me. She's very good at knowing how people are feeling. 'What's the matter?'

'It's my mum,' I said. 'She's ill. She's got to go to the doctor today. She keeps being sick and she's off work and everything.'

'Oh no!' said Yasmin, really concerned. She's a good mate about things like that. She put her arm round my shoulders and we stood looking out through the playground railings at the trees in the park opposite.

'I'm sure she'll be OK,' she said. 'It's probably just a little bug, right? Remember I had one a few weeks ago. I was sick seven times, nearly. But then next day I was better again. Mum said it must have been a dodgy chicken sandwich we bought in the Mall.'

'But Mum wasn't better again today,' I said. 'She was worse.'

'She'll be better again tomorrow,' said Lauren. 'My mum was ill last week, just the same. There's a bug going around.'

I began to feel a tiny bit better. Then, suddenly, Yasmin kind of exploded.

'Wait!' she gasped. 'She's being sick a lot?'

'All the time,' I said gloomily.

'She may not be ill at all!' cried Yasmin with a huge grin on her face. She jumped up and down and clapped her hands. 'She may just be going to have a baby! A little brother or sister, Ruby! Wouldn't that be fantastic? Amaaaaazing! What will you call it? I think Zara's a lovely name, with a Z, but if it's a boy I hope you call it Toby – what do you think, Lauren?'

'I like Scott,' said Lauren. 'If I ever have a boy, I'm going to call him Scott.'

They both stood and beamed at me. I was completely and utterly stunned.

CHAPTER 3
Snap out of it!

THE THOUGHT OF MUM having a baby blotted out everything else. I walked into school like a zombie. I took off my coat, went to our classroom, put down my bag and sat in my usual chair. But I was totally unaware of anything or anyone.

In my mind I was tiptoeing into Mum's bedroom. There was a cot beside her bed. I peered into the cot. A horrible squashed-up pink face peered back up at me. Mum was lying on her bed and staring down in adoration into the cot, and stroking the baby's head.

'Isn't he beautiful?' she sighed, not even looking at me.

'Ruby! Ruby Rogers! Ruby Rogers!' shouted the baby. Whoops, no, it was Mrs Jenkins calling the register. I focussed on her. She looked cross.

'Ruby!' she called. 'I've called your name three times! Snap out of it!'

'Sorry!' I said. Everybody turned round and looked at me. I felt myself going red. I looked down at the table top. Yasmin was writing something on a piece of rough paper. She pushed it across to me.

You could call him Tim, she had written. Tim is Yasmin's favourite name at the moment, because she's got a crush on a boy at Ashcroft High called Tim Moore. She's mad about him, but I think he looks a bit like a meerkat.

I ignored her note. I just glared at the wall. I didn't want to think about the baby having a name. In my imagination he was right there again. This time he was lying on Mum's shoulder, glaring down at me as I stood behind them.

'Take that, you loser!' said the baby and spat a stream of smelly milk all over me.

'Aah, bless him!' said Mum in a stupid soppy voice. 'Whoops! I think His Lordship's nappy needs changing! Run and get a clean nappy for me, will you, Ruby?'

'Yeah,' added the baby with an evil wink, 'and if you're really lucky, you'll get to carry my poo away and throw it down the loo.'

Back in the real world, we were settling down to first lesson. Yasmin was going to give her talk. Mrs Jenkins called her out. Yasmin picked up her notes and walked down to the front of the class. She must have been really nervous. You could see her hands shaking. But I just couldn't focus on Yasmin right now.

In some private hell of mine, my baby brother had already taken over my mind.

'From now on, Ruby Rogers,' he grinned wickedly from the changing mat, 'you are my slave, OK?' And, in that lovable way that only baby boys can, he peed in my eye.

I tried so hard to snap out of my waking nightmare and concentrate on what Yasmin was saying. I could see her mouth opening and shutting as she talked on and on about Allah and the Koran and stuff. But not a word of it entered my head.

'There's my little darling!' cooed Mum, changing his nappy. 'There's my ickle sweety-pie! *Up and down the garden, like a teddy bear . . . one step, two step, tickly under there!* – Pass me those wet wipes, Ruby!'

All that tickly teddy bear stuff used to be mine. Not that I'd want it now, because it was just for babies. But I didn't want anybody else to have it. Especially not the Evil One, my baby brother. He turned his head in my direction.

'Yeah,' he said secretly to me. 'Go and get the wipes, and get a move on, or as soon as I've grown some teeth, I'm gonna bite your neck!'

Mum wasn't the only one to worship at Baby Brother's feet. Dad went all soft and sang songs to him. He sang 'Hushabye Baby on the Treetop' – that used to be my song! 'When the bough breaks the cradle will fall' – yeah, that was my only hope.

Grandma and Grandad came and worshipped him, too. And in my horrid fantasy, Nanny and Gramps came over all the way from Australia and gave him a beautiful pony, even though he couldn't even walk yet. The pony was kept in a field down the road, because our garden wasn't big enough.

'I'm calling the pony Fatbum, after you,' the baby informed me fiendishly when the grown-ups weren't looking. 'And I've got a special job for you that involves shovelling his dung.'

Suddenly a loud noise broke out. It made me jump. It was everybody clapping. For a split second I thought they were clapping what the baby had just said, but then I jolted out of my daydream and realised they were clapping because Yasmin had finished her talk.

'Now, I'm sure we all have questions for Yasmin,' said Mrs Jenkins. 'Let's start with you, Ruby.'

My mind went totally blank. Completely and utterly blank. In my imagination I could still feel the baby's eyes boring into me. I couldn't think of a single question.

'What's – what's your favourite colour?' I spluttered. Everybody laughed, and not in a nice way either.

'Don't be silly, Ruby!' snapped Mrs Jenkins. 'Not that sort of question! A question about Islam, relating to Yasmin's talk.'

I felt like a complete idiot. My face went bright red, but inside my head there was just a white board. A hand appeared holding a crayon. *Loser*, it wrote. It was the baby's hand.

'Oh, for goodness' sake!' sighed Mrs Jenkins. I was *so* not her favourite person today. 'Who has got a question? Hannah?'

'Can anyone become a Muslim?' asked Hannah.

That was an idea. I would become a Muslim. I would go and live with Yasmin's family. I'd be the youngest there, with Yasmin, and everyone would make a fuss of us. I certainly didn't want to stay in my family if it meant being sandwiched between two tormenting brothers.

After a few minutes, Yasmin came back to her seat. I slapped her on the back and whispered, 'You were brilliant!' It took an enormous effort, but I felt I owed her some support. Yasmin wasn't satisfied, though.

Later, when we'd gone out for mid-morning break, she turned to me, pulling a hugely terrified face.

'Wasn't I awful?' she said, cringing. 'Wasn't it boring? Wasn't it absolutely ghastly? Do you think the ending was OK, though? Was it OK? Which bit did you think was OK? If any of it was? Ooooh, Ruby, it was awful! And by the way, why did you ask what my favourite colour was? It was way off the subject. And, in any case, you know it's pink!'

CHAPTER 4
Ruby, don't be silly!

'IT WAS ALL GREAT,' I said. 'It was a brilliant talk. Brilliant.'

'Yeah, but what about that bit about traditional clothing and the veil and stuff?' Yasmin's eyes were huge with anxiety. 'Did it sound OK?'

'Fine, fine, cool, mega,' I assured her, my heart beating fast. I hadn't heard a single word about traditional clothing. I'd been trying to fight my way through a blizzard of nappies – and not clean nappies, either.

'What do you think about the traditional clothing thing?' Yasmin asked me. 'It's OK, isn't it? I mean, if some women want to, that's up to them, isn't it? And if some women don't, that's fine, too, wouldn't you say?' I hadn't the faintest idea what she was talking about.

'I totally agree with you,' I said.

'Do you?' Yasmin's face was right up against mine. Her eyes were huge. 'Because I wouldn't have thought you . . .' Her voice died away. She stared into my eyes for a few seconds. 'Ruby, what's the matter?' she said. Yasmin can tell when something's wrong, even if you try and hide it.

Tears welled up in my eyes. Yasmin immediately gave me a big hug.

'I've told you,' she said. 'Your mum will be fine! She's probably not ill, just going to have a baby.'

'But I don't want a baby!' I protested, trying to fight off the stupid tears. 'I keep having horrid nightmares about this evil baby brother who says mean nasty things to me when the grown-ups aren't looking. And if we had a baby now, everybody would worship him and nobody would care about me any more.'

'Ruby, don't be silly! Listen, I'm gonna get my mum's cheese sandwiches out — that always cheers you up, yeah?' Yasmin scrabbled in her bag. I watched, a tear running down my nose. For the first time ever, I didn't really feel like one of Yasmin's mum's cheese sandwiches. Yasmin just went on giving me a pep talk.

'Anyway,' she said, 'it might not be a boy; it might be a girl. Imagine that! Amazing! Fantastic! A baby girl! We could call her Diamond or Pearl to go with Ruby, and we could get beautiful little outfits for her with sparkly flowers on and stuff. And tiny little pink shoes! And tiny socks with lacy trim! Oh my God! I can hardly wait!'

She handed me the sandwich with a sort of triumphant grin. It sounded as if she was thinking of my baby sister as a kind of superdoll.

I took a bite of the sandwich, but it was hard work eating it. My life seemed to have been turned upside down and inside out, and my tummy felt inside out too.

The rest of the school day was simply dreadful. I was still bothered by horrid thoughts of the baby, and whenever we had a spare moment, Yasmin prattled on about how wonderful it would be when Diamond Pearl was big enough for a skating skirt.

Eventually, about ten years later, it was time to go home. But I didn't really want to go home. Home was different now.

I decided to walk. I would walk very slowly. I knew what was going to happen this evening. Mum was going to announce that she was going to have a baby. How gross! How embarrassing! It was the end of my career as The Youngest. Up till now I'd thought I hated being the youngest, but now I realised I kind of liked it after all.

'Hey! Ruby Rogers! Why the long face, as the cat said to the racehorse?'

I looked up. There, right in front of me, stood Holly Helvellyn and her awful boyfriend Dom. I almost burst into tears on the spot.

I adore Holly. She would be the perfect person

to confide in. But Dom is horrid. Ever since she's been going out with Dom, Holly hasn't really had time for me. And he thinks he's so cool, he doesn't even bother to look at me politely. He kind of sneers down at me from his great height as if I'm a dead rat.

So of course I couldn't tell Holly about the nightmare I was living through. I couldn't tell her about Mum being ill and Yasmin saying it could be a baby on the way. I couldn't say any of that in front of Dom.

'Hi, Holly.' I gave her a smile, but it wasn't a very real one.

'Are you OK?' said Holly, looking closely at me.

I nodded. 'So what sort of day have you had?' she asked.

'Fine,' I said. 'Yasmin gave a talk. About being a Muslim.'

'How interesting!' said Holly. 'Was it good?'

'Mega,' I replied. Dom sort of sighed and looked irritably away.

'Dom's a Buddhist,' said Holly with a proud grin, as if it was yet another sign of his extreme glamour.

'What's a Buddhist?' I asked. I knew about Buddha, of course. My uncle who lives in Bath has a statue of Buddha in his garden.

'Dom's into spiritual development,' said Holly adoringly. 'Buddhists believe that after death we are reborn into another life.' I hoped that in his next life, Dom would be reborn as a slug.

'What do you believe in, Holly?' I asked semi-desperately. 'Do you ever, like, pray?'

Holly looked at me in a searching kind of way.

'Is something wrong, Ruby?' she said suspiciously.

'I'm just asking,' I said, without a smile.

'Well, of course I pray,' she smiled. 'You know – when I'm late for school or whatever. I say, like, *Please make the bus be still there*, and stuff like that. But I'm not sure who I'm praying to – anybody who's listening!'

Dom sighed and looked at his watch as if he thought Holly had spent enough time on me and they ought to be going.

'What I really like, though,' said Holly, 'is doing a tarot reading. Only it's more like a bit of fun. You know, fortune-telling, sort of. I've got a tarot pack. Would you like to come round for a reading some time?'

'Oh yes!' I gasped. 'I really, really need to know what's going to happen in the future!'

'How about tomorrow night after school, then?' asked Holly. 'Dom has his Italian class on Thursdays.' Apparently she was only free when Dom had something else to do. I hope I never have a boyfriend.

'OK,' I said. 'Shall I come round your house, then?'

'Yes,' said Holly. 'I'll meet you after school, if you like.'

This was a tiny ray of hope in my world of gloom. As I hurried home, dreading what I would find there, I sent up a silent prayer: *Hi God, Jesus, Allah, Buddha, whoever – please, please, please don't let Mum be going to have a baby.*

CHAPTER 5
Stop that damned snivelling!

WHEN I GOT HOME, there was nobody there except Joe. He was watching a very loud, very scary film on TV.

'Where's Mum?' I shouted above the noise. He didn't even look at me.

'Gone to the doctor's,' he said, watching the evil thing from outer space destroying Birmingham.

'Where's Dad?' I yelled across the sound of exploding cities.

'Gone with her!'

My heart kind of lurched with alarm. If Dad

had gone with her, this was a give-away. She must be pregnant. I'd seen plenty of TV dramas in which doctors smile at a couple and say, 'Good news – you're going to have a baby!'

I didn't know what to do. Normally when I get home I'm absolutely starving, so I have a snack. But now I felt too anxious to eat. I didn't want to go upstairs and be with my monkeys. It would be horrid to be alone. But I didn't just want to sit and watch aliens destroying the world with Joe. I felt really annoyed with him, that he could watch TV at a time like this.

I went over to the corner where the computer is, and switched it on. It would give me something to do while I waited for Mum and Dad to come home and break the awful news that we were going to have a baby.

Dad is a bit of a news junkie, so he's set the BBC news as our home page. I don't usually take any notice when it flashes up, but this time something caught my eye. *QUINS BORN IN LONDON*, it said. A woman had given birth to five babies! FIVE! Oh my gawd! My heart started to race like mad.

Please God, I thought feverishly, *don't let Mum have quins. Or even twins.* I tried to imagine what it would be like in our house with five babies all yelling. I shut my eyes tight at the horrible thought. All those babies! Mum and Dad would never have time to speak to me ever again. Five lots of dirty nappies! Five lots of feeding! I almost fainted at the thought.

Then I realised something truly awful. Even if Mum only had one baby, I'd probably have to share my bedroom with it. Although we do have a spare bedroom, it's ever so small and Dad keeps all his books and teaching stuff in there: maps and things. It's a real mess.

And if Mum had twins or triplets or quads or something, I'd probably have to get rid of my treehouse-bed platform because it takes up so much space. My room would become like a dorm with a line of nasty little cots. And it would smell like Mrs Fisher's house. She lives across the road from Yasmin and she has babies and kittens peeing and pooing all over the place and it really stinks in there.

If Mum had twins it would be bad enough. They'd outnumber me. They'd gang up on me. They'd borrow my toys and break them. They might even grab my monkeys and rip their heads off! My blood ran cold. In the pit of my stomach

I began to be absolutely certain about something. I think they call it a premonition. I was absolutely sure Mum was going to have twins.

I needed to prepare, and fast. I typed the word 'twins' into Google. I had to know all about twins, so I could be ready for all their tricks. But what I got was so startling, I almost fell off my chair. Conjoined twins! Twins born joined together! Twins joined at the head or at the chest or the tummy!

I just couldn't help looking, the thought was so weird. As I looked, my eyes filled with tears. These poor kids! Joined together for ever with everybody staring at them all the time! OK, so I was staring at them right now, but that was kind of private. Imagine what it's like for them when they go out to the cinema or something!

I vowed there and then that if I ever saw conjoined twins out shopping, I would totally not stare at them. But right now, I was kind of mesmerised. I did a search on conjoined twins. There were pictures of them dating back hundreds of years. Sometimes nowadays surgeons can separate them, but apparently they feel kind of lonely afterwards even if they're very tiny. It's all so mysterious.

Joe's film finished and he switched off the TV with a sudden violent click, and jumped up. I kind of flinched and exited from the pictures of the twins in case he come over and saw what I'd been looking at. I felt really guilty, somehow, and disturbed.

Please God, Allah, Buddha, I thought, *please let Mum not have conjoined twins. And please look after all conjoined twins everywhere and make them have no pain. And please help the surgeons who try to separate them and make them succeed. Love, Ruby.*

I was getting quite religious since Mum had been sick. It's amazing how my life had been totally transformed. Before, I'd been so happy and care-free, even if I hadn't realised it. Now I was on the verge of a nervous breakdown.

Joe had gone out to the kitchen. I switched off the computer and followed him. He was making beans on toast.

'Want some?' he said, opening the tin. Strange, Joe hardly ever makes food for me and now he was offering me something at the very moment when I was sure I would never eat again.

'Yes, please,' I said. I thought if I said no he would get cross and never make food for me in future. My legs felt a bit wobbly from the pictures of the conjoined twins, so I sat down. 'Don't just sit there, you sad sack of fungus!' said Joe. 'Get the spread out. Deal with the toast.'

I got up again and went to the fridge. Joe often calls me a sad sack of fungus, or worse, but this time it seemed cruel for some reason. As I was looking inside the fridge, a couple of tears crept out of my eyes and my nose filled up because I needed to cry. I so wanted Joe to be nice to me, but he just doesn't know how to. In fact, his life revolves around inventing new ways of being hor-rid.

I got the butter out, and when the toast popped

up I put it on two plates and put the spread on.
Joe was heating up the beans. I kept looking down
at the table because I didn't want him to see me
crying. A tear actually splashed down into the
margarine.

'What's the matter now?' he demanded, carrying the saucepan full of beans over. 'Stop that
damned snivelling or I'll lock you in the cupboard
under the stairs!'

'I'm worried about Mum!' I sniffed. 'What if she
has conjoined twins?' Joe sort of froze in mid-air,
with the beans half poured. He frowned at me as
if I was speaking Chinese.

'WHAT???!!' he snapped. At that very moment, my mobile rang in my schoolbag. I scrambled to get it. Somehow I thought it would be a message from Mum and Dad, but it was from Yasmin.

PLS RING ME NOW, RBY! it said. *HORID THING HPPN! HELP HELP PLSE! RING LANDLINE NOW!*

CHAPTER 6

Why would I do such a horrible thing?

I JUMPED UP AND ran to the phone. Something horrid had happened to Yasmin! All the time I'd been messing about on the computer, she'd been having some kind of awful crisis! I dialled her number.

'Yes?' That's the way she answers.

'It's me!' I gabbled. 'Whasshappened?'

'Oh, Ruby!' I heard Yasmin actually burst into tears – really burst, like a balloon full of water or something. 'I've had an anonymous email!'

'A what?'

'An email! From a weirdo! It said, "Your talk was rubbish and you're a bighead!"'

'What?' I was stunned. My head was reeling. 'But it must have said it was from somebody! It always says the sender's address!'

'It was tcxb@hotmail.com.'

'Tcxb? Tcxb? It's got to be somebody in our class . . . Who could it be?'

'I don't know!' Yasmin wailed. 'I've been through everybody in my head and it's just horrible. Sometimes I think none of them could have done it and sometimes I think anybody could have! Everybody hates me!' And she went off into a big sobbing number.

'Yas!' I tried to get past the sobbing. 'Yas! Listen to me! Nobody hates you! Listen! Tell your mum about it!'

'Mum's out!'

'Where's Zerrin?'

'Zerrin's at her dance class!'

'Tell your dad!'

'No, no!' Yasmin's voice dropped to a whisper. 'Dad's downstairs talking to his team about their next job. I can't tell him. He'll get angry and come to school to shout and it would be soooo embarrassing. I can't even tell Mum in case she tells Dad.'

'Well, tell Zerrin when she comes home.'

'She might tell Mum.' Yasmin's sobbing was dying down a bit now. 'I can't tell *anybody*.'

'You should tell Mrs Jenkins tomorrow.'

Yasmin sniffed a bit and sighed a shaky sort of sigh.

'Ruby,' she said in a tiny, tiny voice, 'Forgive me for asking this, but I can't help . . . I mean, I . . . It wasn't *you*, was it?'

'Me?' I exploded. '*Me??!!* Why would I do such a horrible thing?'

'You did send me that anonymous valentine,' said Yasmin with just a slight hint of crossness in her voice. Oh my gawd! That was so true.

'Yas, that was supposed to be just a joke,' I said. 'Anyway, it was only because you'd left me to look after Lauren all by myself when Mrs Jenkins asked us both to.'

'I *so* did not leave you on your own with her!' snapped Yasmin. She loves a row and can jump into one just like that.

'You *so* did!' I snapped back. 'You went off with Hannah and totally left me alone with Lauren!'

'I did not!' yelled Yasmin. 'You went off with Lauren and left me alone with Hannah! You and

44

Lauren were practically best mates! And you waltzed off to have tea at her house and I didn't even get invited!'

'You didn't get invited because she didn't think you liked her! Because you didn't even talk to her or anything! And when we were doing painting in the afternoon, painting our favourite animal, you said her favourite animal looked like a piece of poo!'

'She's the one who's a bighead!' shouted Yasmin. 'Oh my God!' There was a sudden silence. 'I bet it's her! I bet she wrote this! I bet she's jealous because you're my best friend, not hers! You are my best friend, aren't you, Ruby? Oh, please say yes!'

And Yasmin started to cry again. Her moods change just like that. It makes me dizzy sometimes.

'Of course I am!' I told her. 'Of course I am! And no way would Lauren ever do anything like this. She's incredibly gentle and polite and stuff.'

'She *seems* gentle,' said Yasmin grumpily. 'Maybe it's just a front.'

'Don't be silly, Yasmin,' I insisted. 'Lauren could never do a thing like this. She's not jealous of you anyway. She knows you and I are best mates. And she's friends with everybody now. She and Hannah are always going swimming together and stuff.'

'Who is it, then?' wailed Yasmin. 'Oh who *is it*?' And there was another long gust of sobbing.

'Listen,' I said. 'Forward the email to me. Maybe I'll have some ideas. We should ask Zerrin to help. And Holly. We can ask them not to tell your mum and dad. They'd understand.'

'I couldn't bear it if my dad came to school and made a scene.'

'No, listen, it'll be OK.'

'Oh!' said Yasmin, sounding distracted. 'I think Zerrin's coming in now.'

'Great!' I said. 'Tell her about it. And keep me posted.'

'Thanks, Ruby,' said Yasmin. 'Talk to you later. Bye!'

She put the phone down. I felt exhausted. I turned round to see that Joe had completely finished his beans on toast. There was no sign of mine.

'You greedy pig!' I yelled. 'You've eaten mine as well! I hate you!'

Joe got up, a mocking expression on his face. I had never hated him more. He opened the oven door and whisked out a plate.

'Here's your grub, you sad sack of alien dung,' he said. 'I kept it warm for you. I didn't want the rat poison to go off.'

He plonked it down in front of me. It was gloriously, sizzlingly hot.

'Oh,' I said. 'Sorry.'

He pulled a face, walked out and switched the TV on again. Sometimes he never even starts his homework until about ten o'clock. The TV blared out noisily. It was a trailer for a film.

'*And at ten,*' the voice boomed, '*the no-holds-barred action movie is* Guardian Angel, *starring Cynthia Rothrock as an ex-cop who finds work as a bodyguard to a businessman threatened by a psycho killer.*'

Phew! And I thought I had problems! And Yasmin thought she had problems! At least we weren't been threatened by a psycho killer.

Wait! That title again! *Guardian Angel.* What if we really do have guardian angels? I looked round the kitchen to try and work out where a guardian angel would be. I decided she (or he) would be hovering by the ceiling above the fridge.

'Listen, Guardian Angel,' I whispered through a mouthful of baked beans, staring at the air above the fridge, 'if you're really there, please help. Please make my mum not have a baby, or babies, or twins, or anything. And please help Yasmin because somebody's sending her anonymous bullying emails. Maybe you know that already. Maybe you heard about it from Yasmin's guardian angel . . . Are you really there? Send me a sign.'

I waited. The only sound was my tummy rumbling in a haunted kind of way. Then there was a sudden gust of wind, and the front door burst open.

CHAPTER 7
Ugh! No! Get your guardian angel to do it!

WELL, THE FRONT door opened, anyway. It was Mum and Dad arriving home from the doctor's. It just happened to coincide with the sudden gust of wind. But I was really spooked for a minute. I ran out into the hall. Mum was taking off her coat.

'What did the doctor say?' I yelled. 'What's happening?'

'Oh, everything's fine, love,' said Mum. But she looked a bit pale. 'I've just got to have a scan so they can see what's what. Can I smell toast? Have you had your tea?' She went into the kitchen.

Dad was taking his shoes off by the door.

'Believe it or not, I have managed to tread in some dog doo-doo,' he said with a sigh. 'Just take it outside and clean it for me, will you, Ruby?'

'Ugh!' I yelled. 'Naw! Get your guardian angel to do it!' and I ran back to the kitchen.

I had nearly laughed for a moment back there. Dad can make me feel better sometimes. Mum was making a cup of tea. Things seemed totally normal. I ate some of my baked beans.

Joe came into the kitchen. He had switched off the TV. He looked at Mum, and Mum smiled at him. I waited for him to ask how things had gone.

'We've run out of Coke,' he said grumpily.

'I'm not buying Coke any more,' said Mum firmly. 'We've got to be more careful about what we eat and drink in this house. If you want Coke in future, you'll have to buy it yourself.'

'Charming!' growled Joe, and he went off upstairs.

Mum sighed and shook her head. So why had she suddenly got this health food thing into her head? Because of the twins, that's why. She'd been told by the doctor to cut back on the junk food because now she was expecting, she needed to have a really healthy diet.

Not that we eat junk food all the time, but we do occasionally have chips or burgers, things like that. And Dad and Joe have always loved Coke. I hate it because it makes me burp and worse. I stared at Mum as she took out the teabags and warmed the teapot with hot water. I had to say what I was thinking. I had to come clean.

'Mum . . . ?' I asked. It was a good time. The males were not here. It was just Mum and me.

'Yes, love?'

'When you have this scan . . . will they be able to tell if the baby's a boy or a girl?'

Mum's eyebrows almost hit the ceiling, her eyes went wide as windows and her jaw literally dropped. Then she gave a funny embarrassed little laugh.

'Oh, Ruby! You've got the wrong end of the stick, love! I'm not having a baby!'

I was hugely, hugely relieved.

'You're not?'

'No, sweetheart. I'm absolutely sure about that! I hope you're not disappointed?'

'No! No!' I got down from my chair. 'I didn't

want another baby! It's bad enough having Joe!'
Oh thanks, God, Allah, Buddha, and Guardian
Angel, I thought. I felt ecstatically happy. No horrid baby!

'Oh, Joe's not all bad,' smiled Mum. I went across to hug her. 'Although I admit he can be a bit of a monster at times. But he doesn't really mean it.' I threw my arms around her and hugged her hard.

'Ow!' she winced. 'Steady on, Ruby – my tummy is a bit tender, love, not so hard.' I let go instantly. 'That's what the scan is for,' she said, rubbing a place under her ribs on the right-hand side. 'To see what's causing this pain and tenderness. I expect it's my silly old gall bladder. My mum had the same trouble when she was my age.'

Suddenly I realised I had prayed for the wrong thing. It was my fault Mum was ill! I had prayed for it not to be a baby, for horribly selfish reasons. I had so *not* wanted to have a baby in the house that I'd forgotten the most important thing – that Mum should be well.

And now she wasn't! She was hurting! And she was going to have to have a scan. It sounded so serious.

At this moment Dad came in in his socks. He pulled an *I'm disgusting* face. I knew he was going to launch into a whole stream of silly jokes now, to distract us from the horrible scan Mum was going to have.

'I've left my shoes on the doorstep,' he said. 'I'm hoping somebody will steal them, but if not, I'll hose them down later. What's for tea, Ruby?'

Suddenly I realised I should have made tea for Mum and Dad. Joe and I should have made twice the amount of beans on toast. We just hadn't thought of that. I was such a useless horrible loser. Tears welled up from nowhere and ran down my cheeks.

'Hey! Steady on, old girl!' said Dad. 'I was only joking. I've already got a cunning plan involving spuds in their jackets and a bit of salad.'

'What's the matter, Ruby?' asked Mum.

I didn't know what to say. I didn't want her to know I was so worried about her that it was making me cry. So I just said, 'Yasmin's been sent a horrid email, an anonymous one, saying she's a big-head and her talk was rubbish.'

'Oh, how awful!' said Mum. She sounded really angry. 'It was her talk today, wasn't it? I remember now, she told us last week how nervous she was. She must tell Mrs Jenkins, mustn't she, Brian?'

Dad shrugged. He was already scrubbing some jacket potatoes.

'Speaking as a teacher myself,' he said, 'there's nothing like having to deal with a bit of bullying to make you feel like chucking it all in and going to work in a supermarket, stacking shelves.'

'Anyway, love,' said Mum, 'you give Yasmin our love tomorrow, all right? Tell her we think she's wonderful.'

Next day at school was going to be tough. But I suddenly realised what I had to do. I couldn't do anything about Mum being ill, but I could find out who had sent that email to Yasmin. I'd find them, and I'd make them wish they'd never been born.

CHAPTER 8
Oh no! This was the last thing I wanted!

B EFORE I WENT to bed, I checked my email. Yasmin had forwarded the anonymous message. It looked like this: *Your talk was rubish and your a bighead!*

Right away I noticed there was something odd about that word 'rubish'. I did a spell check on it and sure enough, it was spelt wrong. There should have been two b's, like this: *rubbish*. Wow! This was a major clue.

I began to feel a bit like a detective in an exciting murder mystery. Well, it wasn't actually a murder, of course. But it was a mystery. If I could find out who had sent the email it would be a brilliant triumph. Poor Yasmin! It was a hateful thing to do.

Next day I took some special treats to school with me. I know Yasmin loves Jaffa Cakes, so I begged a couple from Mum and wrapped them up for Yas. I also took my cuddly blackbird. If you press its back it sings just like a real bird. Yasmin loves it and I thought she might like to borrow it for a day or two.

I got to school late, though. It was Dad's fault. He'd forgotten all about his smelly old shoes out on the front doorstep and he'd had to clean them up at the bottom of the garden, wearing a pair of very old gloves, which afterwards he threw away.

I went up to Mum's room to kiss her goodbye. She was going to stay in bed today because the pain was still there. She kept shaking her head about Dad's stupid shoes.

'I should have reminded him,' she said. 'I'm not on the ball at all at the moment.'

At last Dad drove me off to school, but by the time we got there the bell had already gone. I raced to the classroom and looked for Yasmin. She wasn't there!

Mrs Jenkins took the register. I started to feel nervous. Why was Yasmin absent? What was wrong?

'Don't worry, Ruby,' said Lauren. 'She's probably just got a bug or something, like your mum.'

'My mum hasn't got a bug,' I said. 'She's got to have a scan.'

Lauren looked a bit worried.

'Ruby, Lauren, pay attention, please!' called Mrs Jenkins. Life was so unfair.

Hannah was about to give her talk about being a Catholic. There were going to be five talks altogether. Yasmin had been first. Then Hannah. Somebody was giving a talk about Buddhism. Debbie Goldman was giving a talk about being Jewish. And last of all, Anil was going to tell us all about being a Hindu.

At the end of the week there was going to be some kind of test. I was already in a total mess about it because I hadn't been able to concentrate on Yasmin's talk yesterday. All I'd been able to think about was that pesky baby, and now it turned out there wasn't even gong to be a baby at all! It had seemed so real to me, giving me evil looks and playing spiteful tricks. But it had all been in my own head. How weird.

Now Hannah was starting her talk. I really ought to try and concentrate on it, but instead I kept wondering if Hannah had sent Yasmin the anonymous email. Maybe Hannah was jealous of Yasmin or something. Or maybe it was because Yasmin was a Muslim and Hannah was a Catholic. I don't like it when the different religions start fighting. They should be setting a good example.

Hannah was droning on about the Virgin Mary and the saints, or something. I was looking at my classmates. Jack Gordon might have done it. He can be quite cruel. Or Rory McKay. He's always teasing the girls.

But wait! I had a clue! Whoever it was couldn't spell 'rubbish'. Maybe I should tell Mrs Jenkins and she could organise a spelling test and there would be the word 'rubbish' in it. Then whoever spelt it wrong would be under suspicion. The trouble is, I don't think many people in my class can spell 'rubbish'. To be honest, if I hadn't done a spell check on it, I don't think I could have spelt it myself.

I went off into a kind of daydream. In the dream our school was a boarding school and we had dorms and everything. One night after lights out, I couldn't sleep. I tiptoed down from the girls' dorm to the IT room, where the computers are. I

could see somebody sitting at a computer at the far end of the room. It was Jack Gordon!

I ran in and he kind of cringed and tried to exit his program, but the screen froze and there, in front of me, was the evidence. He was in his email program and there was an email addressed to Yasmin. It read: *You are bonkers and your hair smells of petrol, you sad sack of sick.*

'So you're the phantom emailer!' I yelled.

He jumped up and tried to escape, but I knocked him to the floor with a mighty uppercut. Just then the lights were switched on by a glamorous IT teacher we had (in my daydream) who looked a bit like Scarlett Johansson.

'Jack's the mystery emailer, miss!' I yelled.

'Oh, well done, Ruby!' said Miss Scarlett. 'Gordon, you can go straight to the head teacher!'

Next day I was awarded a special prize for my detective skills, and Jack Gordon was thrown into the dungeons for ten months. It was that sort of school.

There was a sudden storm of clapping – not for my daydream, but for Hannah's talk. Oh no! I'd forgotten to listen again! Now I know nothing about Islam, and nothing about Catholics either. I do know they have the Pope, and I had a real dream once where I got him all kind of muddled up with Father Christmas.

After we'd talked about Catholicism for a while, we did some reading, and then the bell went for break.

Now was the moment when I'd start my detective work. I remembered an episode of *Poirot* which I'd seen at Granny's. In that, *everybody* was a suspect.

'Lauren . . . ?' I asked cunningly. 'Can you just write something down for me?'

Lauren looked puzzled.

'What for, Ruby?'

'It's just a sort of game,' I said. Lauren didn't

know anything about Yasmin's poison-pen email yet so she wouldn't be at all suspicious. I felt a bit mean starting out on her, but Yasmin *had* wondered last night if Lauren might be jealous of me and Yasmin being best friends.

Lauren picked up her pen. She looked a bit uncertain but sort of secretly smiley, as if it was a game. If only she knew. But really this was just to eliminate her from my enquiries. I pushed a piece of rough paper over to her.

'OK,' I said. 'Write this: rubbish.'

'What?' Lauren can be slow sometimes. 'Write rubbish? Do you mean scribble?'

'No, it's like a spelling test. Write the word "rubbish".'

Lauren thought for a minute, and then wrote it. She pushed the paper back to me. It looked this: *rubish*.

Oh my gawd! She'd spelt it wrong! Right now she was looking at me all innocent and shy as usual, but her spelling had given her away! Lauren was my prime suspect! This was the last thing in the world I wanted!

CHAPTER 9

You must really hate me!

'OK,' I SAID. 'Fine. Let's go out to play.'
Lauren frowned.

'But why did you ask me to spell "rubbish"?' she
asked.

'Never mind,' I said. I could feel myself blushing. 'It's nothing. Just a joke.'

'I don't get it,' said Lauren, puzzled. 'What's the
joke, Ruby? Sorry, I'm being slow.'

'It's not a very good joke,' I said, pulling on my
jacket. 'Forget it! Come on! You can have one of
my Jaffa Cakes.'

I ran out, and Lauren followed me in her clumsy plodding way. How could she have done such a thing? She seemed so sweet and kind on the surface. But you never know what's going on in people's secret imaginations.

If Hannah had looked at me while she was giving her talk, she'd have thought I was listening to her. But I'd been lost in my daydream about the boarding school and Jack Gordon sending poison emails to Yasmin.

I reached the far side of the playground, where Froggo and Max were pulling at each other's clothes in that stupid way boys do. Lauren came puffing along behind me. I got out the Jaffa Cakes. I wished I hadn't offered her one now. As she reached us, I noticed that her eyes were kind of shadowy and shifty.

Lauren had a hidden nastiness, I was sure. A split personality. She was probably really angry all the time, deep down, because she was new at school and she hadn't managed to break me and Yasmin up.

'What was that joke about, Ruby?' she asked.

'What joke?' said Froggo.

'It wasn't a joke,' I said quickly. 'Have a Jaffa Cake.' I held it out to Lauren.

'What about me?' demanded Froggo. His eyes went even bigger than usual.

'I've only got two,' I said.

'You can have half of mine,' said Lauren. She tried to break it in half but a lot of crumbs and bits of chocolate fell on the ground.

'Oh no!' she wailed. 'I'm so rubbish! Here you are, Froggo.'

My heart missed a beat. What had she just said? *'I'm so rubbish!'* Almost exactly the same words as Yasmin's poison-pen email! I felt sick.

Max came up to me. 'If you share your Jaffa Cake with me,' he said, 'I'll tell you a really weird thing I read on the internet.'

'OK,' I said. 'I'll have two bites, and you can have the rest.' I had to try and think about something else. My brain was reeling.

'Ugh!' said Froggo. 'Ruby's gross spit will still be on it!'

'Your spit is way worse than mine!' I snapped. I was desperate to distract myself from the awful idea that Lauren was guilty of writing the email – guilty as hell. 'Your spit is like the slime on old ponds!'

'Your spit is like spiders' sick!' grinned Froggo.

'I don't mind,' said Max. 'I'll have it anyway.'

'You've got a crush on Ruby! Ha ha!' yelled Froggo.

'I have not!' said Max. 'I'm just after her Jaffa Cake.'

I gave him half the Jaffa Cake. I was really annoyed with Froggo for saying cruel things about my spit. And for saying Max had a crush on me. It had made me blush again. I hate blushing. You feel such an idiot.

I was really angry with Max too – for saying he didn't have a crush on me. Although, of course, I didn't want him to have a crush on me. If anybody had a crush on me, I wanted it to be Froggo.

Most of all I was furious with Lauren. Now I'd started to think of her as my prime suspect, everything she did or said seemed suddenly creepy and evil.

'So, who wants to hear my weird thing?' demanded Max.

'Go on, then!' I said. Even though it was unfair because he should really only be telling *me* the weird thing, because nobody else had given him half a Jaffa Cake. But I was getting so cheesed off with the whole pack of them, I couldn't care less.

'A woman in America has given birth to a rabbit,' said Max, grinning.

'That's so not true!' shouted Froggo. 'I know a *real* weird thing.'

'What?' said Lauren.

'If you cut off a chicken's head, it still goes on running about.'

'No, it doesn't,' said Lauren. 'I know because we've got chickens.'

'I know another weird thing,' said Max. 'Some people in America have their heads cut off – after they die, obviously – and they have them stored in tanks, so one day, when scientists have worked out a way of creating new people from old brains, they can be born again.'

At this point Hannah arrived. She was wearing special braids in her hair – probably because of her talk.

'I like your hair,' I said. It wasn't that I'm into braids or anything girly like that, but I hate it when her hair is all loose and she thrashes it about, and if it gets in your eye, it stings like mad.

'Thanks, Ruby,' she said. 'What did you think of my talk? Was it OK?'

'Yeah, it was brilliant,' I said, even though I hadn't actually heard a word. 'Wasn't it, Lauren?'

Lauren nodded.

'It was way worse than Yasmin's, though, wasn't it?' asked Hannah. I think that's called fishing for compliments.

'No,' I said. 'I thought they were about the same.'

'But Yasmin's was brilliant and mine was rubbish,' said Hannah.

Oh no! She'd said *'mine was rubbish'*. And she seemed kind of jealous of Yasmin and her talk. Maybe Hannah had to be a suspect too.

'I prefer Jesus to Mohammed,' said Froggo. 'Because he walked on the water. That is soo cool! He was into water sports! Ha ha!'

Max roared with laughter. Hannah looked a bit upset.

'Maybe he didn't actually walk on the water!' said Max. 'Maybe he had like a kind of hidden surfboard!'

'Stop it!' said Hannah. 'You mustn't talk about Jesus like that.'

'Jesus won't mind,' said Froggo. 'He's a mate of mine.'

'Shut up!' said Hannah. 'Or I'll tell Mrs Jenkins.'

'Grass me up, would ya?' said Froggo in a gangster's voice. 'Just you try. I'm gonna come round yo' house tonight with Jesus, Mary an' Joseph, and we're gonna windsurf all over yo' garden pond!'

Hannah ran off, looking tearful. This was surely the worst break time ever.

'I'm off!' said Max nervously. 'I never saw you, right? I was never here.' He turned into a fighter plane and zoomed away.

'Don't tell Jenko what I said,' growled Froggo. 'Or you're dead meat!' And he ran off too.

'What a nightmare!' I said. 'Everything's going wrong today.'

'Why's Yasmin away?' asked Lauren. 'Is she ill?' She looked so worried, I suddenly remembered how nice Lauren had always been, letting me have tea at her farm and ride her pony and everything. I felt she wasn't guilty of the poison email at all. I was sure it was Hannah now. She seemed so touchy about her talk, and wanting it to be better than Yasmin's.

'I'll tell you a horrid secret, Lauren,' I said. 'I don't know why Yasmin's away, exactly, but she was really upset last night. Somebody sent her a horrid anonymous email, and I think it might have been Hannah!'

Lauren's eyes were suddenly enormous. 'No!' she gasped. 'How could she? Why would she? What did it say?'

'It said, "Your talk was rubbish and you're a big-head,"' I told her. 'But whoever it was didn't spell "rubbish" properly, so that's our main clue.'

I felt better now I'd got Lauren on my side. It's lonely being a private eye and I'd just realised that Lauren could be my sidekick.

But Lauren didn't look too keen on the idea. Instead, she was staring at me in disbelief and kind of backing away.

'Oh, R-ruby!' she stammered. 'That was what that was about, wasn't it? When you asked me to spell "rubbish"? You thought I might have done it! That's so mean! And sneaky!'

'Oh, I didn't really think so,' I said quickly. 'I was just eliminating you from my enquiries.'

'No you weren't!' Lauren's face looked truly ghastly. She'd gone as white as a sheet and she was staring at me as if I was a pile of particularly smelly horse manure. 'You thought I'd written that horrid email to Yasmin! You thought I could do a nasty thing like that! You must really hate me! Oh my gosh!' Her eyes filled with tears and she ran off.

CHAPTER 10
That is so not true!

FOR THE REST of the day Lauren blanked me. In class she sat way over the other side of the room, as far away as possible from my loathsome presence. At lunchtime I tried to get near her so I could explain and tell her I knew she hadn't done anything wrong, but she ran away and locked herself in one of the girls' loos.

There were loads of other girls in there and I didn't want to make a scene by hammering on the door and shouting, *'Lauren! Come out! I didn't*

73

mean it!' So I just walked off sadly and looked for somebody else to talk to.

Max and Froggo were out in the yard, having a shouting match over by the gates.

'That is *so* not true!'

'It *so* is!'

I went over to find out what it was all about.

'I read about it on a website about UFOs,' said Max.

'Yeah! Which is totally, like, invented,' sneered Froggo.

'It's not invented – the governments just want to cover it up. And there are people who've been abducted and the aliens took them away in space-ships and, like, experimented on them and stuff, and then when they came back nobody would believe them.'

'Because they are nutters!' yelled Froggo with a big grin.

'Do you really believe in aliens?' I asked Max.

'Well, I didn't before,' said Max, 'but a couple of nights ago me and my dad saw a UFO and then I read up about it on the internet and there's loads about aliens on there – loads of people have actually met aliens.'

'You're an alien!' said Froggo.

'Well, I'm just off to another galaxy!' shouted Max. 'Human beings are too boring!' And he made a high-pitched noise like an engine revving up and whirled round and round like a flying saucer, and then raced off across the yard.

'Got any chocolate?' said Froggo hopefully. 'Any more Jaffa Cakes?'

'No,' I sighed. 'They were supposed to be for Yasmin anyway, to cheer her up. Guess what! She got an anonymous hate email last night.'

'What?!' Froggo's eyes flared. You could see why he's called Froggo. 'Who from?'

'It was anonymous, you idiot,' I sighed. 'From a false email address with just letters. Like, tcbx@hotmail.com or something.'

'What did it say?'

'It said, "Your talk was rubbish and you're a big-head". But they spelt "rubbish" wrong – with one b. At first I thought Lauren might have done it, but now I think it might have been Hannah. And Lauren won't speak to me because for a while she was my prime suspect, and she found out. I think Yasmin's away because of it. She thinks everybody hates her.'

'I found my Easter egg hidden in my mum's wardrobe last night,' said Froggo, suddenly changing the subject. He was avoiding my girly talk of emotions and relationships – typical of boys. 'Are you having a party or anything at Easter? Can I come round and see your tree house again?'

'I don't know,' I said. 'My mum's ill.'

'My dad was ill once,' said Froggo. 'He had to have his appendix out. They showed it to him afterwards. It looked like a dead man's finger.' This is the sort of thing that passes for conversation when you are with a boy.

The afternoon passed in a haze of torment. Lauren was still avoiding me like a hurt bear. I thought of all the wonderful times I had had at her farm: the pony rides, the lambs and piglets, and her gorgeous little brother Roly, who Lauren says adores me. I felt so sad, it was like having a sack of cement hanging round my neck.

At last the bell went for home time and I switched on my mobile. It buzzed. There was a message: *DON'T 4GET UR COMING TO MY PLACE FOR A 4TUNE TELLING SESSION! LOL HOL X I'LL MEET U AFTA SCHL.*

Holly's tarot-reading invite! I'd totally forgotten! This was ace. It was the best news. I quickly dashed off a text to Mum telling her I was going to Holly's after school. Then I ran and got my coat. Lauren was hanging about by the gate – her mum hadn't come yet. When she saw me approaching she turned her back on me. I ran right past.

I had to make it up to Lauren and be friends again tomorrow. Maybe Holly would have some ideas. There she was, waving at me. I raced up to her.

'Holly!' I panted. 'You look brilliant!' She was wearing a red and black stripy jumper, black and white stripy tights, and a black mini skirt. Her boots were big and had lots of buckles and zips. 'You're all stripy!' I grinned.

'Yes, I'm going to be a zebra in my next life, remember?' said Holly. 'Or a tiger. Come on – I'm starving. What are you going to do for Easter? Are you going to see your auntie in Wales?'

I told her all about Mum being ill, and I nearly cried, but I managed to fight it off and Holly gave me a hug.

'I'm sure she'll be better in time for Easter,' said Holly. 'My mum was ill once. She had to have a hysterectomy.'

'What's that?'

'It means having your womb out. She had to take it easy for a few weeks, but she's totally better now – better than she ever was.'

She held my hand all the way down Waterford Avenue, which made me feel a lot better. We didn't talk for a while. Then, when we got near her house, I said, 'Do you believe in aliens?'

'My dear Ruby,' she said in a pretend posh voice, 'I believe in absolutely *everything*.'

When we got to Holly's house, the first thing we did was ring Yasmin to find out how she was. I'd tried ringing her on my mobile during the day, but she wasn't picking up.

Now we tried the landline and her mum answered and said Yasmin was OK, she'd just had a little headache because she hadn't slept very well. I knew she'd been too upset to sleep because of the mystery email. Poor Yas! I asked her mum to give her my love.

'Will do, Ruby,' said Mrs Saffet. 'I'll tell her you rang – but I don't like to disturb her now, because she's catching up on her sleep.' So that was OK. Thank God Yasmin wasn't really ill.

Then we went up to Holly's room. It was untidy, and there were weird things everywhere: leopardskin-print cushions, dark red velvet curtains, a lamp like a skull and a cute doll who looked like a vampire.

'Now, make yourself comfortable,' said Holly. She drew the curtains and lit two candles. We sat on the floor, on each side of a little sort of coffee table she's got up there. 'Have the leopardskin cushion,' said Holly. 'He's called Leo.' It was just like Holly to have a cushion with a name.

She got her fortune-telling cards out and shuffled them. Then she asked me to shuffle them. I was starting to feel nervous, and my hands were a bit shaky, and the cards kind of jumped out of my hands and lay scattered everywhere.

'Sorry!' I said. 'Shall I start again?'

'No! Wait!' said Holly. 'It might have been meant to happen like that.' My spine tingled slightly. 'Close your eyes and pick seven cards from the heap,' she said.

I obeyed. Each time I picked a card I held it out to her, and I felt her take it from me.

'You can open your eyes now,' said Holly. She'd cleared all the other cards away, and the seven I'd picked lay on the table, face down.

'Wait a min,' said Holly. 'I'm such a dough brain! I meant to burn some incense and play some music.' She got up and went over to her CD player. Some shivery, sparkly music broke out.

'It's Indian,' said Holly.

'I know,' I said. 'I heard some Indian music at the Tandoori House when we went there for Joe's birthday.'

Holly lit a joss stick and stuck it in a little vase. Sweet smoke began to drift through the air. I did-

n't much like the joss stick, to be honest, but it was
Holly's bedroom, so I just tried to keep it out of
my nostrils without her noticing.

'Right,' said Holly. 'Turn over the first card.'

Ohmigawd! It was a picture of a horrid skeleton
dressed in a cloak, riding a horse and carrying a
scythe, and the title was written in kind of sinister
black letters: *DEATH*.

CHAPTER 11
I'm totally confused

'**O**H MY GAWD·!' I yelled. 'It's Death!
Death! Deathdeath! Deathdeathdeath!' I
was flapping my arms about in a blind panic.
Holly reached across and grabbed my wrist.

'Chill, Ruby!' she said firmly. It was as if she was
speaking to a dog. 'It doesn't mean death. Not literally. It does NOT mean death, OK? Nobody's
going to die, I promise.'

'Death!' I squeaked one last time. I'd quite enjoyed
the panic in a way. 'What does it mean, then?'

Holly frowned and scratched her head.

'Uhhh – change. Yes. Change, transformation. A major change in your life over which you have no control.'

'In other words . . .' I trembled. 'Death!'

'Stop shouting death, for God's sake, or I'll strangle you right here on the carpet,' snapped Holly. She was looking a little bit stressy. I made a huge effort, remembered how much I adore her and bit my lip.

'Turn over the next card,' said Holly.

It was the six of coins. She squinted at it. 'Hmmm,' she said, 'to be honest, I've forgotten what this one means. Hang on a minute . . .' She grabbed her tarot book and looked something up.

'Advance, triumph, progress!' she beamed. 'So you see, this change and transformation stuff has got to be good. Next card!'

This time I turned over a card of a king.

'The King of Wands,' said Holly. She looked it up again. I got the feeling that she didn't know her cards all that well.

'Passion,' she said. 'Strong feeling. Fiery stuff. Do we know a man like that?' We both thought hard.

'No,' I said. 'My dad's a wimp.'

'So's mine!' said Holly. 'Never mind. Next card!'

The next one was a rather scary picture of the moon, looking down with a sad face on a dog sitting by a castle.

'Hmm . . . the Moon,' said Holly. 'I think that means delays . . .' She grabbed the book again. *'The Moon remains unclear and distorts reality,'* she read. 'Not very helpful. Except that, errrr . . . you'll have to be patient. Or something.'

The next card was the Devil. I almost jumped out of my skin at his nasty scowly face, black horns and ugly tail.

'The Devil!' I yelled. 'The Devil! The Devil!'

'Shut up, Ruby, please!' Holly seemed to be regretting offering me this card reading. 'The

Devil doesn't represent the Devil. It says: *The price for the journey is revealed only at its end.*'

'What does that mean?' I asked.

'It'll all become clear when you've had all seven cards,' said Holly.

Next card was the Page of Cups. He looked quite cute in the picture, wearing a little mini-skirt thing like boys did in days of old.

'Ah, this means you must go for emotional truth in all things,' said Holly.

I wondered what that meant. So far the cards had only messed up my mind and made me totally confused. I picked up the last card. It was the Three of Swords. I didn't like the look of it much. Holly kind of cringed when it appeared.

'Oh, this one means divorce,' she said.

'I hope Mum and Dad don't get divorced,' I said, a horrid chill running up the back of my legs.

'Of course they won't!' said Holly. 'I think that card's meant for me. I keep getting it when I do the tarot on my own.'

'Do you do it every day?'

'No! Although I did do it four times last week! I get so muddled with the messages! I think I'm addicted. Now Ruby . . .' Holly stared at my seven cards, lying face up.

'Death and the Devil, that's change and delay . . . emotional honesty, strong feelings, fiery stuff . . . divorce, no, ignore that one. And don't forget the Six of Coins: advance, triumph, progress! So more or less encouraging, but realistic, don't you think?'

As emotional honesty was needed, I took a deep breath and shrugged.

'I don't understand a word of it, Holly,' I said. 'I'm totally confused.'

Holly burst out laughing, overturned the table and the cards, and gave me a hug.

'Oh, Ruby!' she giggled. 'You're priceless! It was a total non-event, wasn't it? I mean, there was just no message there at all. It was garbage.'

I shrugged. I didn't want to be rude about her precious cards.

'Do you believe the cards can really tell the future?' I asked. Holly's very cool, but this tarot stuff was all a little bit silly in my view.

'I believe in everything!' said Holly, packing up the cards. 'I believe in miracles! Gods – you name them, I'll believe in them! And goddesses, even more so! Astrology – I'm a Scorpio, what are you?'

'Virgo,' I said, looking grim. 'But that's rubbish too, because Virgos are supposed to be tidy and I'm the messiest person on the planet.'

'Whereas Scorpios are mysterious and charismatic!' grinned Holly. She pulled a mysterious and charismatic face, I think.

'Hey!' she raised her nose and sniffed. 'I smell spuds in their jackets! Come on, Ruby – time for the little pigs to dive into the trough!'

We went downstairs into Holly's super kitchen. I think I love her house more than anybody else's – except ours. Because her mum is so arty, the walls are covered with amazing modern paintings – real ones, full of bright colours. The floor is beautiful honey-coloured wood, and the lighting is amazing – a mixture of those halogen downlighters and spotlights on the paintings, so it's always light and cheery.

'Now, Ruby,' said Holly's mum, getting the potatoes out of the oven. 'What would you like on your potato: butter, cheese and baked beans?'

I nodded happily. 'Yes, please,' I said, sitting down next to Holly.

She picked up a newspaper that was lying on the table and leafed through it.

'Here we are, Ruby,' she said. 'The horoscopes. Here's yours – *Virgo: you're facing a big money crisis unless you are more careful, but for once your mind's not on your purse strings. You'll waltz through today giving off such sexy vibes, every-body will notice.'*

'Ugh!' I groaned. 'Gross!'

'It shows what rubbish horoscopes are,' said Holly's mum, grating the cheese. 'What's mine say?'

'I can't read yours out in public.' Holly grinned. 'It's far too rude. It's about a candlelit dinner followed by a scented bath with your loved one.'

'Well, as Dad's in Manchester,' said Mrs Helvellyn, 'that little caper is certainly not on the cards. There you are, Ruby.'

She placed a wonderful baked potato in front of me, drooling with melted butter and capped with grated cheese.

'We don't have to worry about feeding you too much,' said Mrs Helvellyn, beaming at me. 'You're so skinny! How do you do it?'

'She worries all the time,' said Holly.

'Oh, no.' Mrs H sounded sympathetic. 'What are you worrying about now, love?' My mouth was full of potato.

'She's worrying about her mum who's got gall bladder trouble,' said Holly, grinding black pepper on to her spud.

'Oh dear, that can be very painful,' said Holly's mum, placing a glass of juice in front of me. 'My sister had a bout of that last summer, in France. But she just stayed in bed a couple of days and then she felt better.'

That was what Mum had said would happen. For the first time for ages I began to relax and feel better. I was truly happy, sitting in Holly's lovely kitchen, guzzling my wondrous baked spud.

Holly walked me home afterwards, and we talked about lovely random things, like how birds make their nests and which countries we'd like to live in if we didn't live in England. Holly said she'd have to go and live in Hollywood (for obvious reasons, it was her destiny). I had to opt for Costa Rica because they've got four different sorts of monkeys in the rainforest there.

Holly left me at my gate, and I couldn't wait to tell Mum what a great evening I'd had. I ran up the path and, because I couldn't find my key, I rang the bell. No answer. I rang again. No answer. I could hear Joe's horrible teenage music blaring out, so he was definitely in, but our car wasn't in the drive. Where were Mum and Dad?

I ran round the side of the house, picked up a stone and threw it up at Joe's window. It missed. I picked up another on. This time it hit the window with a loud angry crack sound (although the glass didn't break, thank goodness).

Joe's face appeared at the window. He looked down and saw me, pulled a face like a mad devil and then disappeared. I went back round to the front door and moments later it opened. Joe stood there in his socks, looking crumpled. His hands were covered in paint.

I stepped inside and looked around. It was all suddenly very quiet. Joe had switched his music off on his way downstairs.

'Where's Mum?' I asked anxiously.

Joe gave a curious sniff, turned his back on me and walked into the kitchen. He ripped off a sheet of kitchen roll and blew his nose noisily.

'She's gone to hospital,' he said.

CHAPTER 12
Stop that infernal screaming!

'WHEN? WHY? What happened?' I gasped. My heart was thudding away like a runaway train.

'This afternoon,' said Joe, opening the fridge with strange panache. 'Wanna pizza?'

'Tell me about Mum first!' I yelled. 'What's happening?'

Joe washed his hands, then he took a pizza out of the fridge and switched on the oven. He picked up a kitchen knife and slit the plastic wrap that was around the pizza. Somehow this made me think of a surgeon. I shuddered.

'She got a bit worse this afternoon, apparently,' said Joe. 'Dad rang me to say they were taking her to hospital.'

'What – in an ambulance and everything?'

'I dunno,' said Joe, leafing through a newspaper and picking his nose. 'Probably. I should hope so.'

'Why would you hope so?' I screamed. 'What do you mean?'

'Nothing,' said Joe abruptly. He walked out of the kitchen and into the sitting room. I followed him. He switched on the TV. It was the news.

'In the last year, 100,000 people who went to hospital got an infection,' said the newsreader grimly. *'Of those, 5,000 died.'*

My hair nearly stood on end with shock and horror. Immediately Joe changed the channel. Suddenly we were in the middle of one of those old cowboy movies.

'Did you hear that?' I squeaked. My voice seemed to have gone, leaving only a demented mouse. Joe sighed and said nothing. I ran upstairs to my room.

The door slammed behind me and it was suddenly quiet. I could still hear the TV shoot-out downstairs, but it was distant and muted. The really deafening noise was my heart hammering and my breathing. I was panting as if I'd run half a mile. This was it. I was having a panic attack.

I looked up at my tree house. I couldn't see my monkeys and, for once, they didn't say anything. I was too scared to cry, too desperate to do anything. Suddenly I dropped to my knees. I shut my eyes and folded my hands.

'Please . . .' I begged. 'God, Buddha, Allah, Guardian Angel, Father Christmas, Easter Bunny . . . please make Mum be OK. Please, please, please!'

I went on and on for ages, until my knees started to hurt. Then I stopped praying and just sat on the floor. I leant back against the wall and stared at the carpet. My mind was a complete blank. I was numb. A dozen scary scenarios unfolded before me, like a horror movie on a loop. But in all of them it was the same: Mum was gone.

About half an hour later, or maybe three years, I heard Joe call upstairs: 'Ruby! Pizza!' I got up kind of dumbly, like a zombie, and went downstairs. It wasn't so much that I was hungry – I'd had a great meal at Holly's. That baked potato and all those laughs! It seemed weeks ago, not a couple of hours.

I went downstairs because I didn't want to be alone any more, and if Joe's project was to eat a pizza, the least I could do was be there when it happened.

He'd laid the kitchen table with glasses of juice and everything. I sat down at my place. He carried the pizza, sizzling, to the table. I could see that in theory it must be appetising. But I was on a different planet.

'How much do you want?' he asked.

'A small bit,' I replied.

He cut me a tiny piece and passed it over, then sat down to eat the rest of it himself. I nibbled a bit. It was hard work.

'Do you think Mum will get an infection?' I asked after a while. My voice sounded odd and cracked, like a doll's voice from long ago.

'Bound to,' he said, like a sort of grim joke. He never took his eyes off the pizza. I couldn't work out whether he was upset or not. I hated him joking, but I didn't feel like shouting at him.

I managed to finish my tiny slice of pizza, but it took for ever. Then I watched Joe eat.

He'd left the TV on, and now there was a stupid game show on. From time to time gales of distant laughter came floating through to the kitchen. It seemed horrid and mocking, but I didn't dare to go and switch it off in case Joe wanted it on.

When he'd finished, we loaded the dishwasher in silence. Then, suddenly, the doorbell rang. I jumped out of my skin. Mum! Dad! News! I raced to the door, though I suppose it was really stupid to think it would be Mum, Dad, or news, because Mum and Dad have keys, and news tends to arrive by phone.

I opened the door. Tiffany stood there, all dolled up. She grinned at me. Her lipstick was a horrible shiny mauve colour.

'Hi, Rubes,' she said. 'Is Joe ready?' Joe came up behind me. 'Hi, Joberry.' She grinned. 'Come on, we're late.'

'Plan B,' he said. 'Mum's had to go to hospital.'

Tiffany's face fell.

'No!' she cried in dismay. 'What? Is it the same thing, you know, that she's been . . . gall bladder or whatever?'

'Yeah,' said Joe. 'Dad's gone in with her, so I'm stuck looking after this thing.' He indicated me with a bored toss of the head. Tiffany's face changed again. You could see she was thinking, fast.

'Hey, we could take Rubes with us!' she said, grinning again. 'You'd like to go to a gig, wouldn't you, Ruby? Amazing band – they're called Purgatory. You'd love it. Come on, Rubes, be a sport.'

I walked away, looking for something to kill Tiffany with. Our mum had been rushed to hospital, and Tiffany hadn't even said she was sorry or anything! She hadn't even said *'Don't worry, I'm sure she'll be better soon.'* All she could do was invite us out to a rock concert. How could she imagine I'd *love it*?

I went into the sitting room. The only thing I could see was a bowl of fruit on the coffee table. I don't think anybody's ever been killed with a bowl of fruit, so I gave up my plan to murder her.

Instead I lay down on the sofa and pulled the throw on top of me. I could hear Joe and Tiffany arguing by the front door. I couldn't hear what they were saying because of the TV, and now some cop series was on, just getting to the exciting bit. A chase through darkened city streets . . . a shoot-out in an empty warehouse . . .

Suddenly I was in an empty warehouse. I was running. Somebody was chasing me. My legs got heavier and heavier. They wouldn't move. Then, out of the blue, I was out on a hillside. The hill was shaking. Somebody said, 'It's an earthquake!' I grabbed hold of a tree. The tree came away in my hand and turned into slime.

I was on a mountainside. The whole mountain was shaking. I suddenly realised it was a volcano. It was going to erupt. *Oh help, God!* I prayed. *Help! Guardian Angel, help!*

In the distance I saw a black horse galloping

towards me. The lava was flowing past me now, in great smoking dollops. Was this my guardian angel? The figure on horseback was carrying a scythe – he was wearing a cloak! It was Death! Death off the tarot pack!

'No! No!' I screamed. The figure arrived and reined in his horse. They towered over me. He threw back his hood! But it wasn't the scary skeleton. It was a gigantic rabbit! The Easter Bunny!

But he wasn't the nice friendly, playful Easter Bunny I'd imagined. He was dressed from head to foot in chain mail and sinister black leather, and as he dismounted and turned to me his eyes flashed, black and savage. I started to scream again. He laid his terrible heavy hand on my shoulder, and –

Suddenly I saw the bowl of fruit on the coffee table. Joe was standing over me.

'Stop that infernal screaming!' he snapped.

Oh my gawd! It had all been a dream!

I looked at the clock. It was way past nine. I'd been asleep for ages. I sat up. My face was crumpled. My hair was crumpled. But at least I wasn't facing the Angel of Death disguised as the Easter Bunny.

'Don't just sit there,' said Joe icily. 'I need your help upstairs.'

CHAPTER 13
Brilliant idea! Brilliant!

I FOLLOWED JOE upstairs to his room. There was a smell of paint and glue. He'd never asked me for help before. I wondered if Tiffany was in there as well. But she wasn't. She must have gone home, or gone to the gig on her own. I was glad.

On Joe's work table was one of his model thingies. There was a criss-cross grid made of thin pieces of wood and lots of strings.

'I'm making a mobile,' he said.

'A mobile?' For a moment my brain refused to work. I was thinking *mobile phone*.

'The things that hang from the ceiling?' Joe explained very slowly and patiently, as if I was an idiot. 'It's for Mum when she comes home – oh, she's going to be all right, by the way. Dad rang while you were asleep. They've had to take her gall bladder out but it's only a minor op. Keyhole surgery. She'll be home in a couple of days.'

There was a huge, lovely feeling like a firework display sort of inside my body. I hadn't felt so thrilled since I first saw my tree-house platform. In fact, this was a way better moment than that. This was the best moment of my life so far.

'So she's going to be all right? Promise?'

'Promise,' said Joe. I jumped on him and hugged him as hard as he'd ever been hugged. He unpeeled my arms and fought me off.

'Promising Young Artist Suffocated by Sister,' he said. I knew everything must be all right if he was talking in newspaper headlines again. 'OK, stop the gross displays of emotion and do some work for once,' he went on. 'I want you to paint faces on these.'

He showed me a little line of tiny babies made from some kind of modelling clay. They were cute but, as yet, faceless.

'Is this for the mobile?' I asked. 'Why babies?'

'Because she's a midwife, you idiot,' said Joe. 'There'll be eggs as well, because of Easter. Sometimes the babies will be sort of hatching from the eggs.'

'Brilliant idea!' I shouted. 'Brilliant!' I started right away. I had to be ever so careful not to smudge them. Joe gave me a tiny thin brush to use. I wanted to do a good job. It would be terrible if I messed it up. I wanted the babies all to look different. It was interesting.

I felt better doing the babies' faces than I'd felt for ages. When I'd been at Holly's I'd been having a good time, but it had only been kind of blotting

out my worries about Mum. They'd still been at the back of my mind. In fact, while we were doing the tarot, they'd been at the front of my mind.

Now, up here working in Joe's room, I felt safe again. I was so glad he'd asked me to help. I'd never been allowed to touch his models before, let alone help with one.

I worked until my back ached, and then we heard Dad's key in the lock. We ran out on to the landing and looked down into the hall. He was taking off his mac. He looked up at us and grinned.

'She's fine,' he said. 'It was that blasted gall bladder. They've taken it out now and she'll be home again in a couple of days.' He looked a bit pale and tired, but his smile was real.

We ran downstairs and I hugged him while Joe put the kettle on.

'This calls for a celebration,' said Dad. 'I fancy a hot chocolate – low fat, of course. And I could murder a cheese sandwich.'

Joe did the catering. I was too tired. Joe didn't tell me off for not helping, either. He seemed very mellow all of a sudden. While Dad ate his sandwich, I told him all about Joe's surprise present to welcome Mum home again. Then we went upstairs and Dad had a look at it.

'I think she'll like that,' said Dad. 'We'll hang it above the bed so she can look up at it while she's relaxing and getting her strength back. Make sure those babies are firmly attached, though. I wouldn't want to be hit in the middle of the night by a falling cherub.'

We laughed, then suddenly I yawned. Dad looked at me, then looked at his watch.

'My goodness, Ruby, it's weeks after your bedtime,' he said.

'I know,' I said. 'But I did have a long sleep on the sofa, didn't I, Joe?'

'Oh yes,' said Joe. 'A very long and blissfully peaceful sleep, actually.'

We shared a secret grin at the thought of my screaming nightmare.

Dad went off to ring Grandma and tell her the good news about Mum, and I went downstairs to whiz a quick email off to Yasmin. I wanted to tell her that Mum was going to be OK, and to say I hoped she'd sleep well tonight and be back at school tomorrow.

When I opened my mail program I was surprised to see two messages waiting for me. One was from Lauren and one from Froggo. I dreaded reading Lauren's – I knew she was really cross with me and she might have told her mum or anything and I might be in deep, deep trouble. So I opened Froggo's first.

Listen, it went. *Don't let Yas tell Jenko about the nuisance email. It wasn't Lauren. It was Max! He sez he was only teasing! He sent it cos he's got a crush on her!! Gross or wot? Max and Yas! Wedding bells????? Urgh!!!!!*

I could hardly believe my eyes. Max had a crush on Yasmin! And the brainless idiot had thought she would, like, be *delighted* to receive an anonymous email telling her she was a bighead and her talk was rubbish. Boys! I just don't understand them. If that's how they try and tell you they adore you, what on earth would they say if they hated you?

I summoned up my courage and opened the email from Lauren. I had to apologise to her anyway, so I might as well see how bad she was feeling first.

Dear Ruby, it went, *I'm sorry I was a bit sulky at school today. I've been thinking about it and you were right, it was totally OK and fair for me to be a suspect along with everybody else. But I hope you do believe me when I say sincerely I didn't send that message to Yasmin and I would never dream of doing such a thing. I thought her talk was brilliant. Sorry I reacted badly. Please say we can still be friends and I'll help you find the real culprit. Love, Lauren.*

I whizzed off an email to Lauren straight away, saying sorry myself and telling her the amazing if slightly gross news about Max having a crush on Yasmin.

Last of all I sent a message to Yasmin. It went like this: *Yas, we missed you today. I hope you're OK. Guess what! The mystery email was from Max, who has a crush on you! Nice way of show-*

ing it, huh? My mum was rushed to hospital today and she's had an operation but she's going to be OK.

Apart from that, nothing else happened. Hurry and get well and come back. Lots of love, Ruby – your guardian angel.

Well, if Joe was going to be mine, the least I could do was pass it on.

Read on for a taster of what's to come
in Ruby's next adventure . . .

Ruby Rogers
Tell Me About It

Available now

An excerpt from
Ruby Rogers: Tell Me About It

CHAPTER 1

Stop bossing me about!

'THE WEATHER forecast is brilliant for once!' Mum was gabbling excitedly as Dad started the car. 'Oh, I do love this time of year! Whitsun's the start of the summer, really, isn't it? Ooh, look at those swallows! Bless their little hearts!' Mum has been almost illegally perky since she recovered from her op. It's great to see her so bubbly.

I was feeling pretty bubbly myself. A trip to the seaside! And this was kind of like sneaking an extra summer holiday in, because it was only the end of May and our main summer hol wouldn't be till August.

My monkeys were sharing the back seat with me, of course. There was heaps of room, because Joe wasn't coming with us. He was staying home 'revising for his A levels'. Huh! I know what that means. Watching TV for hours on end and going out to parties with the revolting Tiffany.

I suppose I should have been glad Joe wasn't coming, because it meant I wouldn't have to put up with the torment of constant teasing. But in a funny kind of way, I was sad instead.

'And don't worry about feeling lonely, Ruby,' said Mum, turning round and beaming at me. 'Because Sasha is just the same age as you – oh, I'll just send Deb a text to tell them we're on our way, shall I, Brian?'

'Yeah, go for it,' said Dad. 'I'd text them every five minutes if I were you. Tell them we're just going down Horsfield Road.'

'Shut up, Brian, don't be silly,' said Mum.

I began to go off into a daydream while Mum was texting. What was Quaymouth going to be like? I wondered if there would be an adventure playground with some ropes and platforms. That's the sort of thing I like.

'You'll love Sasha,' said Mum, after she'd sent her text off. 'She's ever such a nice girl. So polite. And guess what! She plays the violin! Plus she already speaks a bit of French – they learn it at St Joseph's.'

Though I was looking forward to meeting Sasha, the news that she played the violin came as a bit of a blow. And I hoped she wouldn't start talking French all over the place. St Joseph's is a rather posh school on the other side of town, so I'd never met Sasha, even though her mum, Deb, is one of Mum's friends at work.

Mum's phone rang. She's just got an ordinary beeping tone. She doesn't bother with any of those fancy ringtones. Mine is the Kaiser Chiefs singing 'RUBYRUBYRUBYRUBY', and Joe's is of chains being dragged about.

'Hello?' she said. 'Oh, Deb! . . . Yes, we've just left. We're just going past Tesco's. Isn't it nice not to have to buy groceries? . . . Yes, I'm sick to death of self-catering. I mean, self-catering's exactly what we have to do at home, isn't it? . . . OK, right, well, have a good journey. See you there! Bye!' She put her phone away and turned to Dad.

'They're already at Warminster!' she said. 'Almost halfway! Mind you, Paul's got a BMW.' I think a BMW is a very flash car. Sasha's dad is a businessman.

'You won't see many geography teachers with a BMW,' said Dad rather sourly. 'I can't help it if they're already at Warminster. You know this old bus won't do more than sixty without overheating.'

'Of course not!' cried Mum, laughing. 'It's not a *competition*, Brian. I wouldn't want to drive fast, anyway. I think it's stupid. I'm very happy to potter down there slowly.'

'Even if it means they'll have first pick of the rooms?' asked Dad slyly.

'Oh goodness, I never even thought of that!' cried Mum. 'It couldn't matter less. Who cares? I'm sure all the rooms are lovely, anyway.'

I started to daydream about Quaymouth. Mum had showed me a picture of the beach, covered with people.

'So what are you hoping to do, Ruby?' asked Mum.

'I want to make sandcastles,' I said. 'And go on walks in woods. And have fish and chips in a cafe. And go for a trip in a boat.'

'What about you, Brian?' she asked Dad.

'My secret plan is to lie in a deckchair for a

week,' said Dad, 'with a handkerchief over my face, while fat women run past in bikinis. Like in the old postcards.'

'Oh, don't be awful!' said Mum. 'You'll want to go birdwatching, I expect – and I'm looking forward to seeing all those lovely old houses. It's where Jane Austen went on holiday, you know!' Mum had packed a load of old books. 'I'm just looking forward to reading for hours and hours – lying on the beach if the weather's warm enough.'

'If the weather's warm enough,' said Dad, 'my main plan is to teach Ruby to swim.'

I felt a bit nervous about this.

I really wish I could swim. Yasmin and Froggo and Max can all swim. Lauren and Hannah go swimming together all the time. But I've always preferred paddling. I can't work out how to wade in deep and let go. It's slightly frightening. If Dad could manage to teach me to swim, that would be brilliant. But I had a secret fear that, somehow, I would never be able to do it. . .

Ruby Rogers: Tell Me About It
is available now!